This book belongs to:
_____
_____

I REALLY want to WIN!

Simon Philip   Lucia Gaggiotti

templar
books

Today is Sports Day. **I can't wait!**
And as I know that I'll be great,
I've planned how I will celebrate . . .

because I'm going to **win.**

All morning I've been training so,
I'm feeling strong, I'm good to go.

I'll take home every prize, you know.

There's **nothing** I won't **win.**

First up, there is a race to run.
The chance I'll lose is next to none.
There's just **no way** I'll be outdone –
I'm certain that I'll win.

I'm way ahead, I've so much speed
my victory is guaranteed . . .

Oh no! I've tripped!

I've lost my lead.

And now I **will not** win.

But, never mind. There's plenty more
for me to win . . . like tug of war!
I've never lost at that before.
This time I'm **sure** to **win!**

I pull with all my **strength** and **might**
and really put up quite a fight . . .

. . . But she is **twice** my weight and height!
There's **no way** I can win.

Look, sports just aren't my thing, okay?
And though things have not gone my way,
tomorrow is a different day.

I'll find **something** to win.

Bake-off!

A spelling bee could spell success . . .
I'm pretty good, I must confess.
If I don't know a word, I'll guess.

BALLET

Spelling BEE

WEIGHTLIFTI

WILLIAM TELL
COMPETITION

DRAWIN

This is my **chance** to **win!**

I've spelled with skill, moved down the list,
but now there comes a shocking twist –
I have to spell ventriloquist . . .

I never, EVER win!

Although that makes me want to cry,
I'll give a different thing a try,
and in the dancing contest I
do **everything** to **win.**

I whirl and twirl, I leap and hop,
I sway and spin and body-pop.
I come to a **flamboyant stop!**

I think that I might win!

But now the other girl's routine,
is deemed the best the judge has seen,
so *she* is crowned the dancing queen.

How does she **always** win?

Collecting prizes, medals, bling
and lifting trophies is **my** thing.

To be the best means **everything.**

I REALLY want to WIN!

So in this game of hide-and-seek,
I've searched for near enough a week.

She has not even made a **squeak!**

I give up trying to win!

But now there is a different prize . . .
and she has *lost*? That's a surprise!
And this is when I realise . . .

she **doesn't** always win.

But strangely, she seems not to mind.
She's come not first but far behind,
and tells the winner, being kind . . .

"You did **deserve** to **win**."

And then she hugs me once she's said,
"You cannot always be ahead.
Enjoy the things you love, instead!

You do not **have** to **win**."

So, as I really love to bake,
I try with all my heart to make
my favourite, most delicious cake –
without a prize to win.

And, actually, I have to say
I've had the most fantastic day!
I don't need prizes anyway
or care if I don't win.

My friend says now she thinks that I
could give one final thing a try.
A competition's caught her eye;
she thinks that **I could win!**

Cake Bake-off!

Bake-off!

This cake display's incredible!
Each cake looks more than edible.
At least my entry's credible –
I can't expect to win.

And now the judging has begun,
but how to pick the cake that's won?
The prize could go to anyone.
They **all** deserve to win!

It's fine to lose. It's quite all right.
The contest is **extremely tight.**

But even so, my friend was right! She told me . . .

For Sallyanne – with heartfelt thanks xx
SP

To Eiril and Tara
I hope this book will always remind you that you win with your passion.
Much Love, Tante Lu
LG

A TEMPLAR BOOK

First published in the UK in 2019 by Templar Books,
an imprint of Bonnier Books UK,
The Plaza, 535 King's Road, London, SW10 0SZ
www.templarco.co.uk
www.bonnierbooks.co.uk

1 3 5 7 9 10 8 6 4 2

ISBN 978-1-78741-411-2

This book was typeset in Brandon Grotesque
The illustrations were created with collage and digital medium

Edited by Katie Haworth
Designed by Genevieve Webster
Production Controller: Nick Read

Printed in China

What do you love to do?
Put your name and
your passion on these prizes.

Congratulations!

First prize in:
....

Name:
....
Winner of:
....

I love to:
....